Wolf Camp

by Katie McKy   illustrated by Bonnie Leick

Tanglewood • Terre Haute

Published by Tanglewood Publishing, Inc., May, 2009.

Design by Amy Alick Perich

Tanglewood Publishing, Inc.
P. O. Box 3009
Terre Haute, IN 47803
www.tanglewoodbooks.com

Printed in the U.S.A.
10 9 8 7 6 5 4 3 2

ISBN 978-1-933718-21-7

    Library of Congress Cataloging-in-Publication Data

McKy, Katie.
   Wolf Camp / by Katie McKy ; illustrated by Bonnie Leick.
        p. cm.
   Summary: After two weeks at an unusual summer camp, Maggie returns home exhibiting some strange behaviors.
   ISBN 978-1-933718-21-7
   [1. Camps--Fiction. 2. Wolves--Fiction. 3. Family life--Fiction.]   I. Leick, Bonnie, ill. II. Title.
   PZ7.M4786957Wol 2009
   [E]--dc22
                                              2008042791

*To my dad, who let me
live with the wolves.
- KM*

*To Doug, my very
own wild child.
- BL*

Maddie showed her mother the flyer.

"Wolf Camp," it said. "Put your child in the wilds."

Maddie was gone for two weeks.

"It's weird here," Maddie wrote home the first day.

"I like it here," Maddie wrote home the second day.

Maddie didn't write home again.

"Oh, she's busy having fun," said her mother.

When Maddie came home, the collie sniffed Maddie, which wasn't strange.

But Maddie sniffed back.

"Hmmm," thought Maddie's mother.

That evening, the collie did what he always did. He begged for food.

Maddie's mother did what she always did. "No!" she said.

Of course, the collie ignored her.

But Maddie's lip twitched. And she growled, which sounded like gravel grinding in her belly.

The collie slunk away.

The next day, Maddie was walking with her mother. A squirrel crossed their path.

Maddie chased.

When she returned, her tongue was flapping.

That evening, a fire truck siren wailed.
The collie howled. Maddie did too.
Maddie sat back, stretched her neck,
and sang the song of the wild.

What was odder still was that Maddie quit eating candy. Instead, she ate only meat: bacon and sausage for breakfast. Hot dogs and hamburgers for lunch, but no buns.

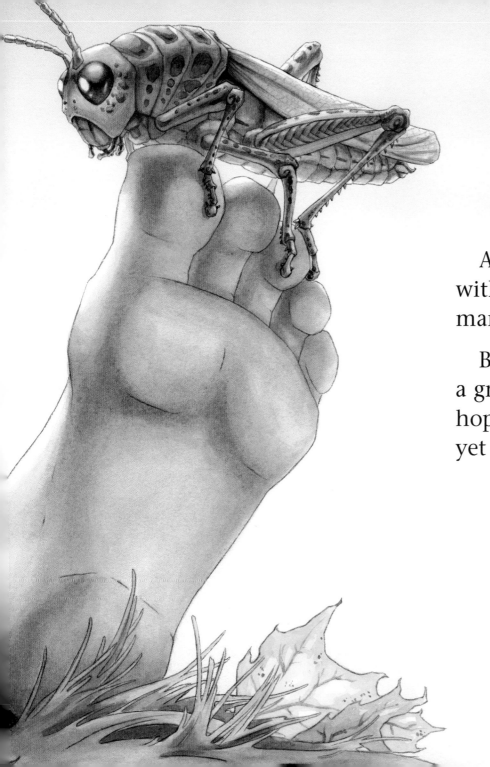

And Maddie snapped at flies—
with her mouth. Luckily she never
managed to catch one.

But one fall day, Maddie did eat
a grasshopper that happened to
hop onto her. It crunched a bunch,
yet Maddie smiled.

Of course, not everything had changed. Maddie
still played tug-o-war with the collie.

She just no longer tugged with her hands. She tugged with her mouth.

And everywhere that Maddie went, she sniffed.
And everywhere that Maddie was, she seemed to hear
things that no one else heard.

She could hear the principal walking down the hall.

She could hear her mother driving down the street,
even when her mother was still three blocks away.

Months passed. Maddie sniffed less. She heard less. She went back to eating bananas and bread and candy. She went back to playing tug-o-war with her hands. And Maddie no longer howled when the fire truck sirens wailed.

"Thank goodness," her mother said.

But the collie never went back to begging.

"Thank goodness," her father said.

For the collie always remembered when Maddie had lifted her lips.

By spring, Maddie was much like any other girl. Except when the collie got fleas, Maddie did too. And Maddie amazed everyone when she scratched her head with her toes.

That May, Maddie showed a flyer to her mother.

"Bear Camp," it said. "Perfect for the wild in your child."

"It's weird here," Maddie wrote home the first day.

"I like it here," Maddie wrote home the second day.

Maddie's mother stocked up on honey and filled the bathtub with fat fish.

"Maybe we'll get lucky and she'll hibernate," her father said.